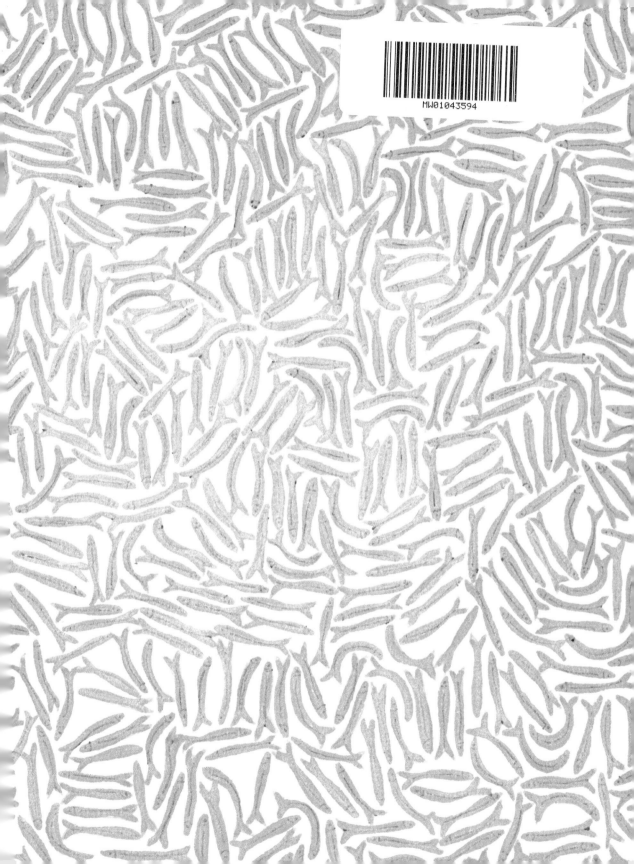

MW01043594

Capelin Weather

by Lori Doody

For my mother, and for Greg

Thank you to Marnie
for helping me get started.

Kate was excited for the start of summer.

But the weather wasn't very good.
The forecast kept calling for

rain, drizzle, and fog.

Cancelled?

Sunny Saskatchewan

POSTCARD

Dear Kate,
The weather here
is great, having
fun, wish you
were here!
 Uncle Steve
  xo

Kate Corcoran
153 Patrick St.
St. John's, NL
A1C 6B8

.50 P

The rest of the country was getting sunny,
summer weather. But here it was just
too wet and too cold for Kate to play outside,
or to do any of her favourite
summer activities.

There was no going on picnics,

no making chalk drawings in the driveway,

no splashing in the pool,

no building bonfires,

and *definitely* no gazing at clouds.

It just looks like a grey blanket.

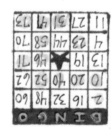

Her grandmother explained that the grey, cold, wet time at the beginning of summer was called 'capelin weather.' She said that it would pass after the capelin rolled in.

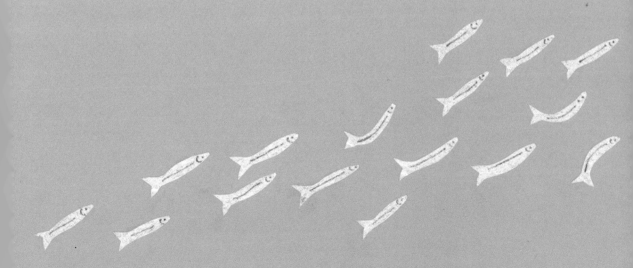

Kate knew that capelin were little fish
that you found on the beach in early summer.
She wondered what they had to do with
the weather. Maybe they rained from the sky…

So Kate watched the sky and the sea
and the shore, but she didn't see any capelin.

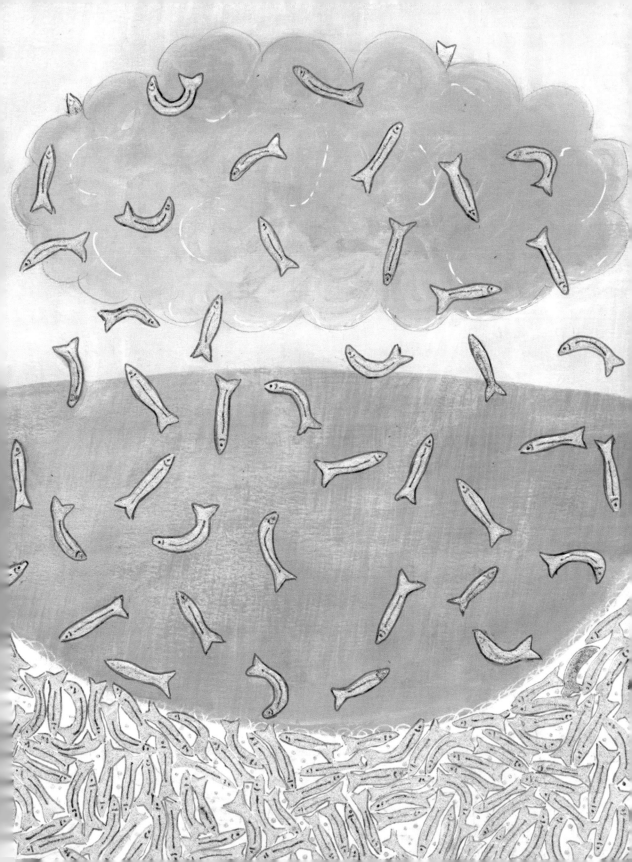

However, she did see icebergs.

She saw whales and kittiwakes.

She saw rain, she saw drizzle, she saw fog,

BRUUUMMME

and even more fog.

Finally, one evening, the capelin were rolling.

The cove became crowded with kids
and grown-ups who all wanted to catch
some capelin. They'd come with dip-nets
and cast-nets, with buckets and bags.

Kate was excited;
she could scoop the capelin up in a pail.

She gave some capelin to her grandmother
for fertilizer for her garden.

She gave some capelin to her grandfather
to fry for his supper.

She gave them a try, but she thought
that they tasted a little fishy.

The next day the weather was much better,

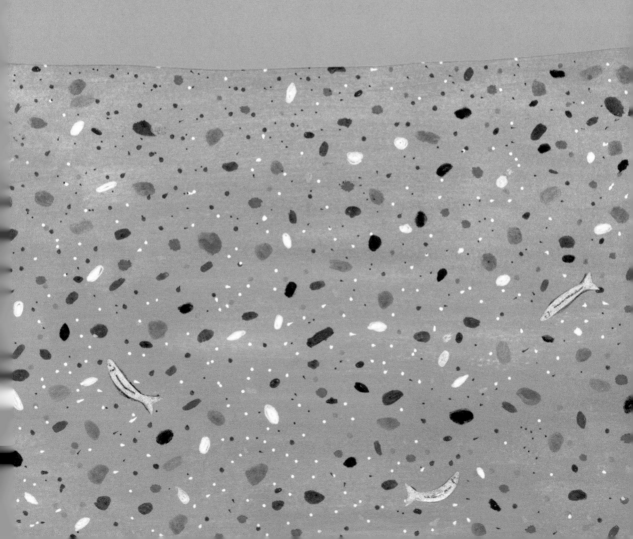

but maybe a little too warm.

Capelin, also spelled caplin, are small, slender, silvery fish
that live in large groups in the Atlantic and Arctic oceans.
They are a vital food source for many sea creatures and sea birds,
including the puffins, gannets, codfish, and whales
that frequent Newfoundland's waters in the summertime.

Kate may have wondered if the capelin rained from the sky,
but they actually swim near the shore and get swept up in waves
that leave some of them stranded on land.

Capelin rolling, or a capelin run, occurs when the capelin
are spawning. Thousands and thousands of these beautiful fish
move into the shallow waters in coves or alongside beaches
to lay their eggs. This is a time of great excitement in Newfoundland:
the whales, and birds, and fish that follow the capelin
are also in close to shore; many Newfoundlanders like to collect
the capelin from the beaches to eat or to use as fertilizer
on their gardens; and maybe, just maybe, there will be an end
to the damp weather.

Capelin weather is the cold, grey, wet weather in late June
and July that coincides with the timing
of the capelin spawning.

The type is Adobe Garamond.
This book was designed by Veselina Tomova
of Vis-à-Vis Graphics,
St. John's, Newfoundland and Labrador,
and printed by Friesens in Manitoba, Canada.

978-1-927917-09-1

Running the Goat acknowledges the Canada Council for the Arts
for its financial support of our trade publishing program.

Canada Council   Conseil des arts
for the Arts   du Canada

Running the Goat
Books & Broadsides, Inc.
54 Cove Road
Tors Cove, Newfoundland and Labrador A0A 4A0
www.runningthegoat.com

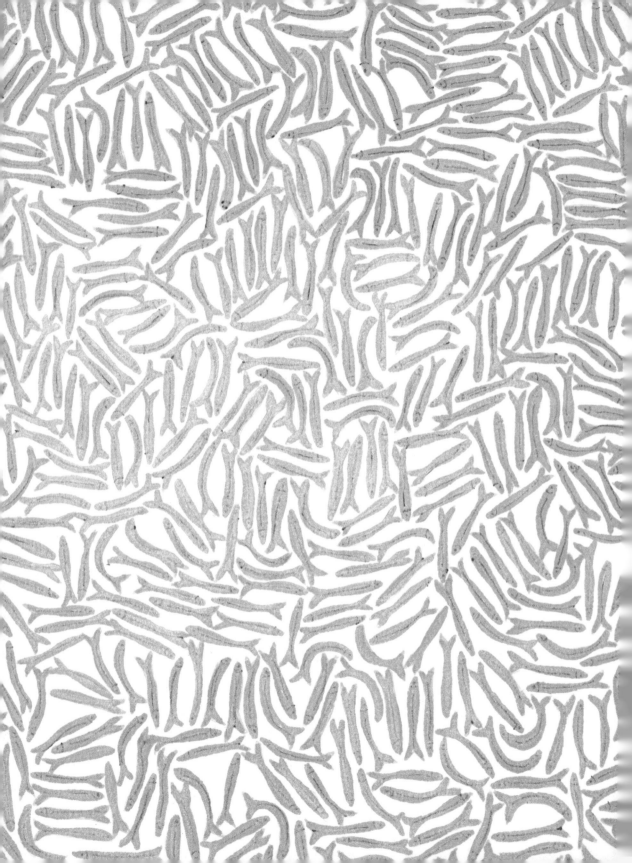